T0198780

AuthorHouse™ UK
1663 Liberty Drive
Bloomington, IN 47403 USA
www.authorhouse.co.uk
UK TFN: 0800 0148641 (Toll Free inside the UK)
UK Local: 02036 956322 (+44 20 3695 6322 from outside the UK)

Because of the dynamic nature of the Internet, any web addresses or links contained in this book may have changed since publication and may no longer be valid. The views expressed in this work are solely those of the author and do not necessarily reflect the views of the publisher, and the publisher hereby disclaims any responsibility for them.

Any people depicted in stock imagery provided by Getty Images are models, and such images are being used for illustrative purposes only.
Certain stock imagery © Getty Images.

This book is printed on acid-free paper.

ISBN: 978-1-6655-8888-1 (sc)
ISBN: 978-1-6655-8889-8 (e)

Print information available on the last page.

Published by AuthorHouse 05/19/2021

authorHOUSE®

Suzie

and

Sam

Suzie and Sam spent their days soaring and swooping over the sea shore.

Below them, people both big and small, enjoyed their day out: chatting, playing and eating.

Suzie and Sam would eat all the tasty treats people would throw for them or leave behind. Chips, bread and doughnuts. All sorts of foods Grandpa Seth would not agree with. As far as he was concerned seagulls should eat fish like they did when he was young.

Some days when Suzie and Sam were feeling very cheeky, they would look out for someone carrying ice creams. They would dive down quickly and carry the ice creams off in their beaks before the people could stop them.

One warm spring day Suzie and Sam set off for a day of soaring and sweeping.

"I would love an ice cream," said Suzie.

"I want a burger," said Sam hungrily.

As they looked down on the usually crowded promenade, something was different. No laughter and shouting from the children playing, no smells from the yummy food that they hunted for. In fact, the seafront was deserted!

"Where have all the people gone and where are all the ice creams?" asked a puzzled Suzie.

All they could hear was the sound of the waves and all the other seagulls flying around confused by the quiet.

Suzie and Sam flew home hungry and confused.

"What's the matter with you two?" enquired Grandpa Seth.

"There are no people on the seafront," Sam answered.

"There are no chips or ice cream either," said Suzie sadly.

As the days went by Suzie and Sam and their friends visited the seashore daily, but it remained deserted.

As Suzie and Sam got home one evening, looking fed up and hungry, Grandpa Seth said, "I tell you what, why don't I take you fishing tomorrow? So you can eat what seagulls should eat!"

"Fish! That's boring," Suzie & Sam answered thinking this day could not get any worse!

The next morning Grandpa Seth, Suzie and Sam got up early and set off to the seashore.

"Come on you two," said Grandpa Seth to a glum looking Suzie and Sam. "You may even enjoy it!"

As the fishing lesson began Grandpa Seth complained, "It used to be so much easier when the sea was blue and there were not all these bottles floating about, but watch what I do and copy me."

Grandpa Seth hovered against the breeze looking for a shimmering shape under the waves. Suddenly he swooped down, his beak disappearing under the water briefly and then he rose back up with a flapping fish between his beak, which he then guzzled down.

"Now you try," Grandpa Seth said to Suzie and Sam.

They took it in turns to dive down into the sea.

They could not manage it at first and then all of a sudden, when they were ready to give up, Suzie rose from the sea with a tasty fish in her beak.

"You did it, you did it!" shouted Sam and Grandpa Seth excitedly!

Then feeling more confident, Sam flew down and proudly rose back out of the water with his first ever catch.

As the days and weeks went by the sea shore was still deserted and the people were nowhere to be seen.

So Suzie and Sam carried on fishing. They were getting better and better every day.

As time went by, they noticed that there were not as many bottles or as much rubbish floating around and the sea was much clearer, which made it easier to fish.

They could also fly faster and longer and didn't feel as tired as they used to, as they were eating healthy food in a clean environment.

Spring turned to summer and then one day, when Suzie and Sam went on yet another fishing trip, they could hear, in the distance, the old noises they used to hear.

The sounds of chatting, playing and eating filled the air again.

The people had come back!

Suzie and Sam perched on a railing. "The people have come back," said Sam, wondering where they had been.

Suddenly a man threw a few chips at them. "I bet you've missed these," he said.

Suzie and Sam looked at each other. "Not really," they said to each other.

And with that they flew up into the sky and over the shiny blue sea for some tasty fish.

THE END

Printed in the United States
by Baker & Taylor Publisher Services